DRACULA

Retold from Bram Stoker's novel and illustrated by
TOM BARLING

GW00715378

CORGI BOOKS
A DIVISION OF TRANSWORLD PUBLISHERS LTD

A CORGI BOOK 0 552 98008 0

First publication in Great Britain

PRINTING HISTORY
Corgi edition published 1976

Corgi Books are published by
Transworld Publishers Ltd,
Century House, 61-63 Uxbridge Road,
Ealing, London W5 5SA

Filmsetting by Photoprint Plates Ltd
Rayleigh, Essex
Originated and
Printed in England by
Westerham Press Ltd
Westerham, Kent

CHAPTER ONE

Jonathan Harker's Journal

AFTER a long train journey from Vienna I arrived in Bistritz, an interesting old town. It lies to the extreme east of Transylvania and near to the borders of Moldavia and Bukovina, in the midst of the Carpathian mountains; one of the wildest and least known portions of Europe. The town has had a stormy existence over the centuries and shows marks of it, having withstood siege by the Turk and been ravaged by fire on five separate occasions.

I booked into the Golden Krone Hotel according to the instructions of my senior partner, and was civilly received by the proprietor and his wife. When they had established that I was 'The Herr Englishman, Jonathan Harker' they handed me a letter which read as follows:

My Friend, Welcome. I am anxiously expecting you. Sleep well tonight. At three tomorrow the coach will leave for Bukovina, a place has been booked for you. At the Borgo Pass my carriage will await you and bring you to me. I trust that your journey from London has been a happy one, and that you will enjoy your stay in my beautiful land. Your friend, DRACULA.

The proprietor had also received a letter from the Count with money and instructions to arrange this last part of my journey. But when I asked him for more details about the Count and Castle Dracula he pretended not to understand my German, he and his wife crossing themselves fearfully. I went to my bed where I spent a restless night for wolves howled in the surrounding hills until daybreak.

The following morning I was visited by the proprietor's wife who begged me not to continue my journey. When I told her that I must for my business was of great importance, she said:

'It is the eve of St George's Day. Do you not know that

tonight when the clock strikes midnight, all the evil things in the world will have full sway? Do you know where you are going, and what you are going to?'

As I had not slept well, her words did nothing to warm my spirits. She was in evident distress, throwing herself to her knees and imploring me not to go. I told her gently that I must, helping her to her feet. She took the crucifix from her neck, hanging the rosary about my shoulders before I could refuse, and left me to await the coach.

There was a considerable crowd around the inn, all made the sign of the cross and pointed two fingers toward me. One of my fellow travellers grudgingly explained that the gesture was a charm against the evil eye. I had never before met such superstition. Many of the people called after me as the coach pulled away, such words as 'vrolok' and 'vlkoslak'. I found the words in my polyglot dictionary and they meant the same thing in Slovak and Servian; *Vampire!*

The horses pulled us away from the town at a good clip, the driver's whip cracking in the crisp air. The road curved and twisted through a sloping land full of forests and woods, many of the trees covered in fruit blossom, scenting the air. We swept along at a great speed as the driver urged the horses on. The road rose more steeply as we progressed, high crags and peaks all around, the higher ones still white with winter snow, the sky heavy with rolling cloud. The sun began to set and the temperature dropped.

The falling sunset threw strange shadows through the pine stands and the rocky valleys, an unsettling effect that showed in the faces of the other passengers. The driver bowed over his reins, demanding greater exertion from the labouring horses. The coach swept over a high ridge and down into the darkness of the Borgo Pass.

The passengers pressed odd little gifts on me, crossing themselves and making the sign of the evil eye as they passed me sprigs of garlic, a twig of mountain ash, a small cross of dark metal. I was both touched and filled with dark foreboding. The night was upon us as suddenly as a thrown cloak, the wind cold and keen, howling like distant wolves; the atmosphere heavy with the sense of thunder.

The horses came to an abrupt halt, steam rising from their hard-driven flanks. They whinnied and shied nervously. There was no light ahead, no lamps showing save those on our own coach. The driver leaned down toward me, his face barely showing in the gloom, and said:

'There is no carriage here. The Herr Englishman is not expected after all. You will come with us to Bukovina, and return tomorrow or the next day; better the next day.'

The horses began to snort and neigh and plunge wildly, so that the driver had to hold them up. Then, amongst a

chorus of screams from the passengers, a carriage pulled
by four horses, drew up beside us. The horses were coal-
black and spirited, driven by a tall man in a great black
hat which seemed to hide his face from us. I could only
see the gleam of a pair of very bright eyes, which seemed
red in the lamplight. He said to the driver:

'You are early tonight, my friend.'

'The English Herr was in a hurry,' stammered the
driver.

'That is why you tried to carry him on to Bukovina. You cannot deceive me, my friend. I know too much, and my horses are swift,' said the tall man, smiling with no trace of humour. The lamplight showed a hard mouth with very red lips, sharp teeth as white as ivory.

One of the passengers whispered, 'For the dead travel fast,' and crossed himself, shrinking away from the window. The tall man lifted my luggage from the coach and helped me to the ground, his grip on my arm showing prodigious strength. I stepped up into the carriage and was thrown back in my seat as we galloped away into the night, leaving the coach far behind in moments, high rocks sweeping past on both sides, powdered snow whipping at my frozen face. I feared I should never again see England or my beloved fiancée, Mina. It was with a great effort that I regained my composure, for the peasants' fears clung to me as heavily as my cold clothes.

We hurried on at the same great pace and were soon hemmed in by towering trees that arched over the roadway, closing us away from the sky. Though we were thus

sheltered, the rising wind moaned and rushed, crashing the branches together, shaking ice from the boughs and whipping the snow everywhere until all around was covered in a white blanket. The howling of wolves was carried to us on the gusting wind, closer and closer.

The trees gave way to the starker shapes of great frowning rocks as we climbed higher, ever higher. There were dips in the road into which we rushed, only to climb more steeply at the other side.

The moon, sailing through black clouds, appeared beyond the jagged crests, and by its light I saw that a ring of wolves kept pace with us, tongues lolling and amber eyes hungrily watching. They no longer bayed, their grim silence more terrible as they stalked us, loping easily through the driving snow. On and on they came, gaining with each stride until I could see the ice in their fur, the golden flecks in their pupils; frosty breath clouding between their bared fangs. It seemed only a matter of time before they were near enough to pull down the lead horses and that my end was close.

The driver stood upright in the madly swaying coach, one arm up and gave an imperious command. The wolves halted and melted away into the shadows as though they had never been there.

A heavy cloud passed across the face of the moon so that we were again travelling in complete darkness, so dark in fact, that I may well have slept. I cannot tell for certain, the journey had been like some awful nightmare. I was suddenly aware of the driver pulling the horses to a halt in the courtyard of a vast ruined castle, the broken battlements dim against the sky, no light showing from the tall black windows. Dark archways led off all around, the fitful moonlight showing no details.

The driver helped me down and led me to a great old door, studded with large iron nails, and set in a projecting doorway of massive stone. I could see in the dim light that the stone was massively carved, though worn by time and weather. As I stood, the driver jumped to his seat and whipped the horses into one of the dark openings. I called after him but my cry was swallowed by the wind. I asked myself, was this the place for an English solicitor? Here, in the wild Carpathians, when I should be awakening from this mad dream in my own home with the bright dawn showing through the curtains?

A heavy step approached behind the heavy door, the gleam of a lamp coming through the chinks in the ancient wood. A chain clanked and massive bolts drew back. A key turned with the loud grating sound of disuse, and the great door swung back.

CHAPTER TWO

Jonathan Harker's Journal

A TALL old man stood in the doorway, an antique silver lamp held high, throwing long quivering shadows as the flame flickered in the draught of the open door. He was all in black, not a speck of colour about him anywhere, his shape distorted by the uncertain light. He made a gesture of welcome with his right hand and spoke in a voice that carried through the wildness of the night:

'Welcome to my house! Enter freely and of your own will!'

As I stepped forward he gripped my hand with a strength

that made me wince, an effect that was not lessened by the fact that his hand seemed as cold as ice, more the grip of a dead than a living man. I said:

'Count Dracula?'

'I am Dracula. And I bid you welcome to my house, Mr Harker,' he said, drawing me inside. He placed the lamp on a bracket, plucked up my bags as though they weighed nothing, and led the way along a vaulted passage, up a winding stair, along another great passage. Our steps rang heavily on the stone flags.

He threw open a heavy door, ushering me into a well-lit room where a table was set for supper and a great log fire flared in the hearth. We passed through this room to a door that led through an octagonal chamber with no window of any sort, and into the bedroom where a fire sent a hollow roar up the wide chimney. The Count set my luggage down, and before withdrawing, said:

'I trust that you will find all you need to refresh yourself after your journey. When you are ready, come to the other room where you will find your supper prepared.'

The warmth of the Count's greeting and the cheerful blaze of the fire quite restored my spirits, dissipating all my doubts and fears. I found that I was famished, and after making a hasty toilet, went to the other room. My host was standing to one side of the great fireplace. He waved graciously at the table, inviting me to eat my fill and to excuse him for not joining me since he had dined earlier. I handed him the sealed letter which Mr Hawkins, my senior partner, had entrusted to me. The Count read it as I helped myself to the excellent roast chicken, cheese and salad that lay before me, and poured myself a glass of old Tokay.

The Count finished reading and looked at me gravely before speaking.

'You are a young man, Mr Harker,' he said, 'but it seems that Mr Hawkins has great regard for you, sending you on such an important mission. He says as much in his letter. He intimates that my affairs could not be more discreetly handled by any other of your profession. I am heartened by his trust.'

'It was only his ill health that prevented him from serving you personally,' I said.

The Count asked me many questions about my journey, and I told him by degrees all I had experienced. Later, we drew chairs up to the fire and I smoked a cigar that he offered me, he himself explaining that he never used tobacco. As we talked I had the opportunity to observe him more closely.

His face was strongly aquiline, a high bridge to the thin nose, the nostrils arched, the forehead loftily domed with the hair scant at the temples, yet profuse elsewhere. His eyebrows were massive, almost meeting over the nose. The mouth was fixed and thin-lipped, and his upper teeth protruded over the lower lip, peculiarly sharp and white against the ruddy lips. His chin was broad and strong, the cheeks thin though firm. His skin had an extraordinary pallor.

His hands were white and coarse with broad squat fingers. Strange to say, there were hairs in the centre of the palm. The nails were long and cut to a sharp point.

He leaned toward me at one point and I drew away from him. His breath was rank and a feeling of nausea overcame me. The Count noticed my discomfort with a grim smile and moved back to his side of the fire. We were both silent for a while, and as I looked toward the window I saw the first dim streak of the coming dawn. From the valley below came the howling of many wolves. The Count's eyes gleamed, and he said:

'Listen, the children of the night. What music they make.' Seeing the strained expression on my face, he added, 'A city dweller cannot enjoy the feeling of the hunter,' and with this strange remark he rose to his feet and suggested that I must be ready for my bed, bidding me a courteous good night. I made myself ready for sleep, my mind filled with the dread wonders of all I had seen. I slept long and soundly, well into the following day.

I dressed and went to the room where we had taken supper. The table was laid with a cold breakfast, a pot of coffee warming on the hearth. There was a card on the table on which was written:

I have to be absent for a while. Do not wait for me. D.

When I had finished eating I looked for a bell to summon the servants to clear away. I could not find one. Another odd deficiency in this most odd household. All

around me was the evidence of great wealth, the table service of beautifully wrought gold, the immaculate antique tapestries, the curtains and upholstery, the hangings on my bed, all of the costliest fabrics. And yet no sign of servants, nor anywhere a mirror or looking glass. I had had to shave and brush my hair with the aid of my travelling mirror. The only sound I had heard had been the distant cry of wolves.

Many of the doors were locked, but I found a library off the dining room. There were many volumes and magazines in English. I was browsing through these when the Count returned, greeting me heartily. He hoped that I had spent a restful night and was pleased that I had found my way to this room.

'These books have been good friends to me. I have studied them for years past, ever since I had the idea of going to London. I look to you, my young friend, to help me to speak your language.'

'Indeed, Count,' I said, 'you speak excellently.'

He bowed gravely.

'Not so,' he said, 'one word from me in London and I should be known and marked as a stranger. That will not do. Here I am noble, I am *boyar*; the common people know me, and I am master. I am not content to be a stranger in a strange land, to be marked apart. I have been master here too long to be anything less. I would be master still—to make certain that none shall master me.'

His face took on an extra pallor, his eyes the colour of blood. Then he smiled, and as his lips ran back from his gums the sharp teeth showed out strangely.

'This is Transylvania and not England. Our ways are strange and not your ways. You have learned enough to know how strange. You may go anywhere you wish within the castle, except where the doors are locked. There are reasons for this, reasons only I can see and recognise. You understand?'

I assured him that I did and would comply with his wishes.

'We must talk at length so that I may learn your English intonation. You will tell me when I make an error, however small,' said the Count. 'And now, you must tell me all about my new estate in London.'

I excused myself and went to my room to collect the papers from my bag. Whilst I was placing them in order I heard the table being cleared in the next room, and as I passed through, noticed that the lamps had been lit, for night had come on. The lamp was also lit in the library where the Count sat reading an English Bradshaw's Guide. I spread the papers and the Kodak views out for him to see and said:

'The estate is near Purfleet and called Carfax, no doubt a corruption of *Quatre Face,* as the house is four-sided, agreeing with the cardinal points of the compass. It contains some twenty acres and is surrounded by a high wall of heavy stone. There are many trees and a small dark lake. The house is large and has been added to over the centuries. The older part is Mediaeval, built in stone with only a few windows, all barred and very high up. There are many rooms, almost too many to count. There is also an old chapel or church close to the main wing. There are few houses close to hand, the nearest is a private lunatic asylum and cannot be seen from the grounds.'

When I had finished, he said:

'I am glad it is old and big. I am from an old family, and to live in a new house would kill me. It takes centuries to make a house habitable for one such as I. Mine is not a heart that seeks mirth or sunshine, that is for the young and gay. The wind breathes cold through my castle where the battlements are broken and the shadows are many. I love the shade where I may be alone with my thoughts.'

I could not help but shudder at the malignance of his smile. He seemed not to notice, but went on to examine the deeds and papers in great detail, asking me many questions about the place and its surroundings. It was clear that he had studied the area and knew more than I did. When I remarked on this, he answered:

'Well, my friend, I shall and must know as much as I can. For when I arrive there, you, Jonathan Harker, will be miles away in Exeter, working at the law with my other friend, Peter Hawkins.'

Then, making his excuses, he left me for a while, asking me to return all the papers to their folder. He was away for some time, and I began to look at some of the books around me. I found an atlas, which opened naturally at England, as though from much use. Certain places on the map had been ringed. One was east of London, his new estate; the other two were Exeter, and Whitby on the Yorkshire coast. Strangely, Mina, my fiancée, was visiting Whitby with her close friend, Lucy Westenra. I put it down to rare coincidence.

The night was well advanced by the time the Count returned, and I was glad to accept his invitation to eat my supper. As before, he did not eat or drink himself. He asked questions on all conceivable subjects, hour after hour. I was not in the least tired, for my extended rest had quite refreshed me, although I was affected by the dawn's rising, for the room became chill and the atmosphere clammy. The shrill of a cock's crow brought the Count to his feet with apologies for having kept me talking through the night and, with a courtly bow, he left me.

I slept little, for my mind was troubled by bad dreams in which my beloved Mina was threatened by some foul thing that came from the sea. Something that came under the cover of dark storm clouds, never clearly seen.

I got up, hung my shaving glass near the window, and began to shave. A hand fell on my shoulder and the Count's voice said, 'Good morning.' I started violently, for the whole of the room behind me was reflected in the mirror, and I could not see him there. In starting I had cut myself. I turned the mirror from side to side but there was no error. Although the man stood close to me, there was no reflection of him in the glass! I turned to face him, much shaken and filled with uneasiness at his closeness to me.

When the Count saw my face, his eyes blazed like hot coals, his fingers reaching for my throat. His fingers brushed the rosary beads that held the crucifix around my neck. He drew them back, his face calming as if the demon had never looked out through his eyes. He snatched up my shaving-glass, hurling it from him through the open window. It fell to the courtyard way below, shattering into a thousand pieces.

'A foul bauble!' he hissed, turned on his heel, and left me.

I searched for him later, but he was nowhere to be found. I roamed the passages and tried many doors, all were locked and barred. The awful truth dawned on me: I was a prisoner.

I must have lost my reason for a time, for I ran hither and thither like a rat in a trap, but to no avail. There was no door that was not barred, no window that did not look out onto a precipice. I found myself in a gallery that was open to the sky, looking out over a sheer drop of a thousand feet to the green tops of the forest below, broken here and there by deep chasms where the silver thread of a river ran. No mortal man could scale that wall of rock and live. God help me, there was no way out. I was trapped.

CHAPTER THREE

Jonathan Harker's Journal

I HAD covered vast distances within the castle by the time the sun was high, and from my exertions during the night, felt drugged and dizzy. I had forced my way through a door in one of the upper galleries and found myself in a great hall hung with decaying tapestries, the shelves lined with rotting books and scrolls. Decades had passed since this wing had been inhabited, only rat trails disturbing the gathered dust near the skirtings. I slumped in a heavily carved chair and fell asleep.

The day had long gone when I awoke with a start.

The air was alive with sparkling motes of light, shining dust that swirled with no breeze to stir it. I went across to a tall window and looked out. I was far above a rough track that led up to the castle walls. A woman's keening reached me from the ground below, and a figure, her dress whipped by the updraught, shook a thin fist up at the great bulk of Castle Dracula. She screamed for her stolen child, sobbed and cried some more, finally trudging away into the gloom of the forest's shadow, her cries as thin as the wind.

I leaned weakly against the cold stone and was overwhelmed by a sense of helplessness. There was no comfort in my surroundings. A movement along the battlements caught my eye, a swirl of darkness in the colourless overcast. It was the Count climbing through a gap in the stones way off to my left, head down and moving toward the ground with incredible alacrity, sliding over the stones like a huge lizard, his great cape billowing around him. He was like a bat on the rough bark of a twisted oak, as sure as a beast on the sheer drop, moving with incredible speed. The sight was both fearful and fascinating. The angle of the wall cut him from sight and I stepped away from the window to sink into the chair exhausted.

The motes in the air swirled brighter and brighter, forming into three distinct shapes that shivered, growing tall and solid. I watched through half-closed eyes as though asleep. In the moonlight opposite me were three young women dressed in ancient finery. They threw no shadows nor did their small feet leave prints in the dust. Two of them were dark haired, the other fair, their faces pale and their noses aquiline like the Count's. Their brilliant white teeth shone like pearls against their livid ruby lips, eyes as pale as sapphires, their laughter and whispering as silvery and tinkling as water-glasses played by a cunning hand. They moved around me as gracefully as white cats, closer and closer. Something commanded me to sleep and forget, forget and sleep.

The fair one approached me, leaned close, gloating horribly, licking her lips like an animal. She arched her neck and her breath was hot against my face, sickly sweet and repellant. Her sisters hissed as her sharp teeth clicked near my throat, her mouth brushing the sensitive skin. I had no will of my own. I closed my eyes and waited with beating heart.

My eyes opened as another presence made itself felt. The Count, his face distorted, gripped the slender neck of the pale sister and drew her away. Her teeth ground together, the fair cheeks suffused with dark blood. The Count's eyes blazed red as with a sweep of his hand, he hurled the woman from him, motioning to the others to keep away; an imperious gesture. The sisters cowered,

hissing. The Count's voice, though pitched low, cut through the air as he said:

'How dare you touch him, any of you? This man belongs to me! When I have done with him you shall kiss him at your will. Now go, I must awaken him, for there is work to be done.'

The women joined together in soulless laughter, the joy of fiends. The fair sister pointed at a bag the Count had thrown to the floor.

'Are we to have nothing tonight?' she hissed.

The bag moved as though there was some living thing in it. If my ears did not deceive me there was a gasp and a low wail, as of a half-smothered child. The Count nodded and the women closed around. They used no door to leave with the dreadful bag. They simply seemed to fade into the rays of the moonlight and pass out through the window. Their shadowy forms showed against the night before they faded entirely.

Then the horror overcame me, and I sank into unconsciousness.

CHAPTER FOUR

Jonathan Harker's Journal

I AWOKE in my own bed. There must have been something wrong with my mind, for I could only accept what I had witnessed as a terrible dream. The Count must have carried me to my room and laid me to rest. The only signs of strangeness was that my clothes were folded differently to my usual habit, and my watch was unwound. Had the Count found this journal I am sure that he would have destroyed it. The thought of those terrible women filled me with aching fear.

Many things became clear to me. It must have been Dracula himself who had met me at the coach and brought me to the castle. It must have been he who prepared the food and made up my bed. There were no servants, just he and I the only living things in this dread place. When I returned to the door that I had used to enter the other wing where I encountered the three sisters, I found it closed. It had been driven so forcibly against the jamb that the wood was splintered. I should never pass that way again.

That evening the Count was courtesy itself. He suggested that I write to my partner to inform him that I should be returning very soon, and to mark the letter as though it had been sent from Bistritz. I did so. When I returned to my room I found that all my papers and documents had been removed along with my travelling clothes and all my money. I tried the door of my room and it was locked from the outside. With that letter sent to my partner my fate was sealed. He would assume that I had left the castle and perished far away from home. I resolved straight away to make my escape. The only way out of the castle was down the sheer walls. I felt that I would rather be dashed to pieces on the crags below the walls than to have the very life sucked from my veins by Dracula and the awful sisters. As I sat with my thoughts the Count let himself into my room. I told him that I should like to leave for England at once. His smile had no trace of warmth or humour.

'I regret, my young friend, my coachman is away on a mission and will not be available to you.'

'Then I shall be pleased to walk,' I said.

Dracula threw back his head and gave out a terrible laugh. He snatched up a lamp and told me to follow him. We passed through the twisting passages until we reached the main door. He threw back the huge bolts and opened the door wide, his arm up in a gesture of command. From all around came the sudden howling of many wolves. They came leaping and snarling across the dark court-yard, teeth champing and hackles raised. 'Could you survive amongst them?' questioned Dracula, only his body between me and the ravenous beasts. I shook my head. Dracula slammed the great door and ordered me to return to my room.

'You can only leave under my protection,' he said. 'I shall tell you when your time has come.'

Back in my room I was in a rage of despair, thoroughly unnerved by the Count's demonstration of his power over wild things. I became aware of whispering outside my door. I threw open the door to find myself facing the three sisters.

'Your time has not yet come. Wait. Wait. Have patience. Tomorrow, tomorrow night is yours!' they whispered in unison. Then they joined in a low and mocking ripple of laughter, running away into the darkness. I closed and barred my door. The agony of waiting for morning taxed my nerve to breaking. The long hours passed slowly until dawn finally showed in the sky and a cock crowed from far off. I stepped out onto the window ledge and lowered myself over the drop.

My feet found easy purchase in the gaps between the great stones where the mortar had been worn away. Down and down I clambered, until I found myself outside a window that looked in on an old cloister leading to a chapel. I climbed in and forced the chapel door. When my

eyes became accustomed to the gloom I could see that dust lay everywhere, the roof a mass of cobwebs. Heaps of gold coins lay everywhere in careless heaps as if they had lain untouched for centuries, many times a king's ransom.

There were many long wooden boxes filled with earth, about fifty in number. The air was heavy with the cloying stench of old earth.

In one of the boxes lay the Count, a sight that filled my soul with terror. His hair was dark and sleek, his youth renewed. The white skin of his face seemed ruby-red beneath, the mouth redder than ever, for gouts of fresh blood ran from the lips and down over his chin and neck. The deep burning eyes were set in swollen flesh, for the lids and pouches beneath were bloated. The filthy creature was gorged with blood. There was a mocking smile on the bloated face which seemed to drive me mad.

This was the being I was helping to transfer to London, where, perhaps for centuries, he could satiate his blood-lust among the teeming millions; to create an ever widening circle of semi-demons to prey on the helpless.

I looked for a weapon. The only thing to hand was a shovel that had been used to fill the boxes with the old earth. I lifted it high and brought it down with all my strength across the hateful face. As I did so, the head turned, the blazing eyes full on me. The sight seemed to paralyse me, and the shovel turned in my hand and glanced from the face, gashing the forehead. The flange of the blade caught the edge of the opened lid and closed the face away from my sight. The last glimpse I had of that face filled me with weakness, a grin of malice that came straight from hell. I shook from head to foot.

Footsteps sounded from outside, the sound of gipsy singing. I turned away from the great box and hid in a dark corner, beneath a stone bier. Many men entered and began nailing the boxes closed and taking them out to load them on carts. The journey of the fiend was about to begin and I was helpless to stop it. I resolved to escape once the gypsies had left with the last of their foul cargo. God trust that I may survive to warn my fellow country-men of their danger. But will they believe me?

CHAPTER FIVE

Mina Murray's Journal

24th MAY: *I have not heard from Jonathan since his last letter from Bistritz, Transylvania, posted in April. His partner, Mr Hawkins of Exeter, has written to tell me not to worry since Jonathan travels in a land where post is not carried so easily as here. My work as an assistant school teacher keeps my mind occupied through the day, but the long evenings are quite another matter.*

30th MAY: Mr Hawkins has sent me a copy of a letter he has received from Jonathan. It baldly says that he is leaving for home. It reads strangely, mentioning nothing of his work there, nor any postscript for me. I am badly distressed. Lucy Westenra has invited me to spend the holiday with her on the coast. I have written to accept.

24th JULY: Lucy met me at Whitby station and took me to the house that she and her mother have taken for the summer. I am to stay as long as I wish and I am glad to be in such company. Lucy has surrounded herself with a group of personable young men. They all seem to be in love with her. There is Doctor Seward who is 29 and the director of a private insane asylum; his close friend, Lord Arthur Godalming, and a charming American from Texas, Mister Quincy P. Morris. They are gay company and keep me

*thoroughly amused when they visit. Mr Morris's use of the
new slang is diverting, although he is careful not to use it
in Mrs Westenra's hearing, for she would be scandalised.
They all do what they can to stop me fretting about Jonathan.*

*4th AUGUST: Still no word from Jonathan. Lucy and I
spend a good deal of our time on the cliffs overlooking Whitby harbour. We sit in the gardens near the parish church
and yard where many seamen lie at rest, looking out over
the picturesque shipping. It is the nicest spot in Whitby, for
it lies over the town, and has a full view of the harbour,
across the bay to where the Kettleness headland stretches
out into the sea. There is a lighthouse on each arm of the
harbour walls. Between the two piers of the harbour mouth
is a narrow entrance that widens into safe water suddenly.*

A sharp reef runs out from the south lighthouse for about half a mile and is guarded by a bell buoy which swings in bad weather, the bell tolling mournfully.

There is an old man, Mr Swales, who tells us many stories about his experiences at sea. He has many tales about sea-monsters and wrecks; although these incidents are frightening when related, we cannot help but listen in shocked delight. He predicts the weather and is invariably correct. He has told us that a storm is likely before the week's end. The coastguard, who holds conversation with us on occasion, overheard Mr Swales say this and did not disagree. Looking out at the sparkling sea under a clear sky it is hard for Lucy and I to believe them.

6th AUGUST: A wind has sprung up out at sea, tumbling surf over the shallows and the sandy flat, its roar, muffled by the sea-mists. The fishing boats had raced for the safety of the harbour. The coastguard has kept watch on a strange ship through his eyeglass.

'I can't make her out,' he told us; 'she's a Russian by the look of her; she seems to see the storm coming, but can't decide whether to run up north in the open, or put in here. Look there again! She is steered mighty strangely, for she doesn't mind the hand on the wheel and changes about with every puff of wind. We'll hear more about her before this time tomorrow.'

8th AUGUST: A great and sudden storm has been experienced here. The approach of sunset had been beautiful, the sky streaked with red and purple, the breeze from the sea off-setting the sultry day. Black clouds massed over Kettleness and lightning danced around the foreign schooner that stood offshore. The waves rose in fury, rising up and smashing over the sea wall, battering against the cliffs. A furious wind brought in blinding banks of sea fog. A new searchlight that had been set up on the East Cliff was set to work by the officer in charge, and swept the sea to aid the fishing boats. Cheers went up from the people on the shore as each craft reached safety. Before long, the searchlight picked out the schooner approaching, all sails set. Between her and the port was the great reef. The schooner swept in so fast that it seemed certain that she would break her back on the rocks. The rolling fog covered her as the darkness thickened.

The searchlight was trained on the narrow entrance, hoping that the light might guide the schooner in if she cleared the reef. The wind bellowed so loudly that the bell buoy could not be heard. The wind changed quarter, clearing a gap in the fog, showing the schooner as it swept through the harbour entrance. A gasp and cries of dismay came from the onlookers, for lashed to the helm was a corpse which swung with the wheel at each motion of the ship. No other form showed on deck. The schooner ran in without pause and drove herself up onto the sand beneath East Cliff, straining every timber, half her top rigging smashing to the deck.

As the ship beached herself a massive dog sprang from below, crossed the deck and bounded ashore, losing itself in the intense gloom beyond the searchlight's beam. It showed briefly among the tombstones in the churchyard before disappearing entirely.

The coastguard and the doctor went aboard the schooner where they examined the corpse. They agreed that the man must have lashed himself to the wheel, tying the knots with his teeth. The ropes had cut his wrists to the bone. Around his neck was a cross and rosary, in his pocket a watertight bottle with pages of his log inside. It is written in Russian and will have to be translated before light can be shed on this strange and awful affair. A thorough search of the ship revealed that there was no other living person on board.

9th AUGUST: The storm has abated as quickly as it came. The derelict schooner is a Russian from Varna, the Demeter. Her cargo is ballast, silver sand and a number of great wooden boxes filled with mould. The local newspaper has gone to great lengths to report this whole affair very fully. The Russian consul has been called to take possession of the ship and to pay the harbour dues. The cargo was consigned to a local solicitor, Mr S. F. Billington, who went aboard this morning to take possession of the boxes. A clerk of the Russian consul has translated the log. It tells of the crew disappearing one at a time in mysterious circumstances. The first mate had talked of a strange man aboard, a fiend. He had tried to open the boxes; then, de-

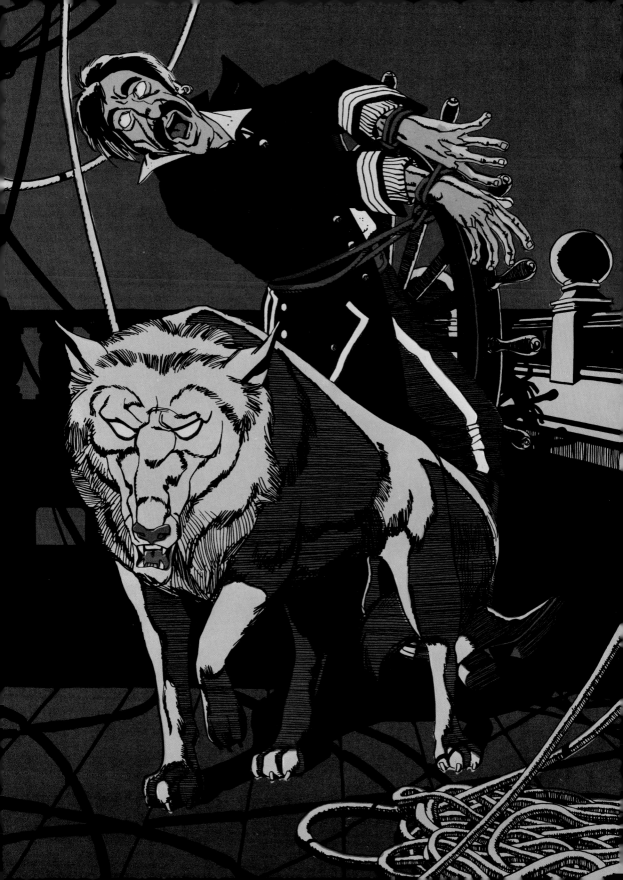

mented with fear, had thrown himself into the sea, leaving the captain alone with his ship. Whether the captain did away with his crew whilst demented, or there is some other explanation is not clear. The local seamen intend to give the captain a Christian burial. He is something of a hero to them.

A search has been set up by the local S.P.C.A. for the dog that came ashore. They fear that it may have made for the moors and want to befriend it before it becomes a danger. A mastiff owned by a local coal merchant was found dead in the road this morning. It had been fighting and was badly savaged.

10th AUGUST: Lucy has taken to walking in her sleep and I keep close watch to see that she doesn't wander off and harm herself. The schooner captain was buried today. Just before the ceremony old Mr Swales was found dead with a broken neck, a look of fear and horror on his face that the men said made them shudder. They think that he must have slipped on one of the churchyard stones. I wish that Jonathan were here.

11th AUGUST: I am so tired. Lucy wandered off in her sleep last night. I awoke with such a feeling of dread that I could barely catch my breath. I searched the house before going out into the bright moonlight. I ran along the north terrace and along to the West Cliff. From there I looked across to the East Cliff, and there, on her favourite seat sat

a white figure that could only be Lucy. It seemed that a dark figure leaned over her, man or beast I could not tell. I flew down the path calling Lucy's name. I toiled up the steep steps and was breathless when I reached the top, my legs trembling.

The dark figure raised its face, very pale with gleaming red eyes. I ran on to the entrance to the churchyard and lost sight of the seat for a moment. When I reached Lucy she was alone, breathing raggedly and shuddering. I put my shawl around her shoulders, pinning it around her throat. I must have been careless for there were pinpricks on her neck, a drop of blood on her collar. She moaned and put her hand to her throat. With some difficulty I got her home, supporting her most of the way. I locked her in her bedroom and took the key away with me.

12th AUGUST: Twice I heard Lucy trying to leave her locked bedroom. I went to her and there was a huge bat fluttering outside the window. It flew off when it saw me. I closed the curtains and Lucy slept soundly until the morning.

13th AUGUST: Lucy stayed in her room all day. She seemed listless and has no appetite. I locked her room early and took an evening stroll along the sea front. As I returned to the house I could see Lucy at her window, her eyes were closed. By her, seated on the window-sill was something that looked like a good-sized bird. I ran up to her room, fearful that she would catch a chill, and put her back to bed without waking her. She looks so pale and wan. The twin wounds in her throat do not seem to be healing. I shall have a doctor tend to them if they are not better soon.

18th AUGUST: So much has happened in the last few days that I have had no time to write my journal. I have received a letter from a Belgian hospital run by nuns. Jonathan has been admitted there and is gravely ill. I am to go to him and bring him home. He has no memory of his travels. Doctor Seward has been in constant attendance on Lucy. He has a great Professor with him from Amsterdam, Abraham Van Helsing. He seems to know what ails Lucy and I leave her in good hands.

CHAPTER SIX

Doctor Jack Seward's Journal

MINA'S letter asking me to attend Lucy Westenra filled me with alarm. Doctor Van Helsing, my old friend and tutor, accompanied me to Whitby. Mina warned us to expect a marked change in the beautiful Lucy, but I was hardly prepared for her gaunt appearance. She was deathly pale, the colour had gone from her lips and gums; her breathing was painful to see and hear. Van Helsing examined the marks on her neck very carefully. When he told me that her condition was due to massive blood loss

I could hardly believe him. He insisted that she must have a transfusion immediately.

I offered myself as a donor but Van Helsing thought that Lord Godalming, her fiancée, should be given that right. Arthur agreed readily and we transferred as much as we dared after Van Helsing had quietened Lucy with a mild narcotic. We were gratified to see an improvement in her colour and breathing. Van Helsing was grim, his face as rigid as marble.

He opened his bag and brought out a garland of garlic flowers and placed them around Lucy's neck, hanging similar wreaths over the window and the fireplace. Then he placed a silver crucifix on the wall over the bed. He secured the windows, rubbing the sashes with a handful of the white flowers so that the room was filled with their scent. It all seemed grotesque to me and I said so. Leaving Lord Godalming to watch over Lucy, Van Helsing led me into the sitting room.

'Tonight,' he said gravely, 'there must be a watch around the clock; and every night until we find the source of the evil that afflicts her. We cannot be too careful, my friend.'

'But doctor,' I said, 'you sound as if you were exorcising some demon. You are a scientist, how can you believe such superstition?'

'I have had experiences of such matters in the past. I have learned not to mock. Europe is old and many of its legends are based in fact. You English put too much faith in the Dover Straits. The old demons have crossed the water and are here. We are all in danger,' said Van Helsing, his kind features hard, his eyes fiery.

'What are you telling me? Quincy and I have experienced the vampire bats in our travels across the Pampas but these are small and feed on cattle and wild beasts.'

'I have questioned Mina. She has told me what has happened here. She has seen the beast that feeds on Lucy. She does not suspect the truth. We must remove Lucy to your asylum where we can watch her more easily. We will leave Lord Godalming and Mrs Westenra to watch over her tonight. You and I must make our travel arrangements from our hotel. Come, we will say our goodnights.'

We were at our hotel supper when Quincy Morris arrived. I left the table to greet him and asked him why he was here. He told me that he had received a letter from Mina before she left for the continent, and the news that Lucy was ill brought him to Whitby post-haste. He had gone straight to the house and had found it in total darkness and his banging had not roused the servants. My heart was gripped by a chill fist. I hurried Quincy into the restaurant to repeat what he had told me to Van Helsing.

We raced back to the house.

There was no answer to our knocking and shouting. We went around to the back of the house, and using one of Van Helsing's surgical saws, I cut through the bars, opening the sash with a thin knife. The servants were slumped in the living room, breathing heavily as though drugged. The air was heavy with laudanum. We ascended to Lucy's room and opened the door.

Lucy and her mother lay on the bed, the older woman half-across her daughter. I felt for a pulse in her wrist. There was none, her heart had failed. Lucy breathed heavily, pale lips curled back from her teeth; whiter and sharper than I remembered them. She was barely alive.

Lord Godalming lay below the shattered window in fragments of shattered glass, some of them flecked with bright blood. There was a livid black bruise on his forehead and he groaned when I lifted his head. Van Helsing attended to Lucy, gently easing her out from beneath her dead mother. She had stripped the garland from her throat and the marks there were mangled and gaping. The terror in Mrs Westenra's face was awful to see. On the floor by the bed, clear in the moonlight, was the bloody pawmark of a wolf.

Lord Godalming responded to smelling salts and opened his eyes; staring wildly he said, 'The wolf! It smashed through the window. The air was filled with specks of light that gathered near the bed. I moved toward it as I reached out an arm . . . I was struck down.' He sank back and shook his head as though to clear it.

Lucy sat up slowly, her eyes opening, bright and luminous as fine crystal. She licked her lips, her tongue running across her sharp teeth. Lord Godalming raised himself up and she turned her hard gaze upon him, her

44

breath hissing in her throat. She held her arms out to him, saying:

'Arthur! Oh, Arthur my love. Come. Kiss me!'

Her voice was startlingly different, soft and voluptuous.

'Mein Gott!' said Van Helsing.

Lord Godalming stepped toward the transformed Lucy, ready to accept her embrace. Van Helsing swooped at him, hurling him away from the bed with furious strength.

'Not for love of your immortal soul,' he said. 'And hers!'

A spasm of rage flitted like a shadow across Lucy's face; the sharp teeth champing together. Then her eyes closed and she sank back against her pillow. She gave a light gasp and was silent, her breast still.

'It is all over,' said Van Helsing. 'She is dead.'

Quincy and I led Lord Godalming from the room. Van Helsing followed us after a moment and said, 'It is not over. It is only the beginning.'

We all stared at him without comprehension.

'She is one of the Undead,' said Van Helsing.

CHAPTER SEVEN

Doctor Jack Seward's Journal

MINA and Jonathan arrived back in time for poor Lucy's funeral. Jonathan's experiences have changed him dreadfully. He is thin and nervous and Mina does not let him out of her sight, a perfect nurse and wife to him. They had married in Belgium and will make a handsome couple when Jonathan is restored to health.

Lucy and her mother were laid to rest in the family vault at Highgate. Death seemed to have restored Lucy's beauty; lying in the open coffin surrounded by candlelight she seemed only to be sleeping. Van Helsing has placed garlic flowers in amongst the lilies, a silver cross on her breast. Lord Godalming was badly affected and could hardly believe that she is gone. Van Helsing and I had to support him through the memorial service. We were a depressed group as we waited for the carriages to carry us from the cemetery to the funeral breakfast.

As we stood in the light drizzle, Jonathan went pale
and would have staggered had Mina not been holding
his arm. He pointed a quivering finger across the road to
a carriage where a man sat under the shadow of the
canopy. His was not a good face, cruelly sensual, his red
mouth open to show his sharp teeth; his eyes the colour
of blood.

'It is the man himself,' said Jonathan, his eyes wild.

Van Helsing was at his side instantly. Jonathan's eyes
rolled up and he staggered against Mina. I started across
the grass to approach the stranger but he whipped up his
horses and wheeled away down the hill at a mad clip.
Jonathan had sunk into a deep sleep induced by brain
fever, a condition I had observed many times. Van Helsing brooded all the way back to the Westenra's town
house, muttering to himself in his own language.

When we arrived at the house, Van Helsing gathered
us together in the withdrawing room and spoke to us
gravely. Jonathan had come to with no memory of what
had caused his fainting spell.

'My young friends,' said Van Helsing, 'you must believe me when I tell you that we are all in the gravest peril. We must all be very brave if we are to prevail over the evil that surrounds us. I know that none of you is truly convinced of this. With Madam Mina's permission I shall attempt to prove it to you.'

'By Timothy,' said Quincy, 'if you can shed light on this affair, I for one should like to hear what you have to say. I shall not rest until I have settled with the fiend that has taken Lucy from us.'

'What do you suggest?' Mina asked Van Helsing.

'I mean to mesmerise Jonathan,' said Van Helsing, 'if you will agree. I must open his mind. His experiences in Transylvania, that dark country, will show us the awful truth.'

Mina dipped into her purse and produced a small notebook, holding it out to Van Helsing.

'But I have his journal,' she said, 'the only thing he had when he arrived at the nun's hospital. I brought it to show you and Doctor Seward, thinking it might help you to effect a cure for his brain fever. It reads like a nightmare.'

Van Helsing opened the book and scanned the first pages very quickly; softly he said, 'It is true. All of it. I should like to read it aloud to our friends. It will help them to understand.'

Mina agreed, and Van Helsing read the whole journal through to us. As he read, Jonathan sat up and watched the doctor intently, his eyes clearer than any time since his return. I felt a chill when Van Helsing reached the part about Carfax, the house in Essex, for it stood close by my asylum for the insane. The thought of Dracula working his will among my patients filled me with horror. Their violent natures strengthened by this man's strange powers would produce demons too terrible to contemplate. I was convinced that we must do all in our power to bring Dracula down; a similar resolve showed in my friends' faces. There was no need for any of us to speak our feelings. The room was electric with our joint intent to avenge Lucy and the other innocents who had fallen before the vampire. Van Helsing stood very tall and very straight.

'Jack and I have dark work to complete this night. The rest of you must stay together. Tomorrow we shall all journey to Essex and Jack's asylum. From there we shall work to destroy Dracula before he can spread his cloak of evil further.'

'Whatever your work is,' said Lord Godalming, 'it shall not be done without me at your side.'

'Nor I,' said Jonathan, his voice strong and resolved.

'You'll not leave me behind,' said Quincy.

'But you must all stay here,' said Van Helsing. 'It will need all of you to keep Madame Mina from harm this night. Only surgeons can do what must be done. Jack and I must go alone.'

'By the powers,' said Quincy, 'wolf, man or bat, he shall feel the keenness of my Bowie knife if he comes against me.'

'You are brave, friend Quincy,' said Van Helsing, 'but at night, Dracula is at his strongest. You must put your faith in the garlic flower and the power of the cross. You must stay together in a sealed room guarded as I describe if you are to live through the night, believe me.'

'We shall do as you say, Van Helsing,' said Lord Godalming. 'Dracula shall not work his evil here.'

It was just on dusk when Van Helsing and I arrived at a small church near Hampstead. I waited in the carriage as Van Helsing went inside to keep an appointment that he had made. It was fully dark when he emerged carrying a small package. His face showed grim pleasure as he put it into his instrument bag. We continued through the night to Jack Straw's Castle where we dined in company with a noisy group of touring cyclists.

It was well after eleven when we left the inn and walked the tree-lined road across the top of the Heath. As we went on we met fewer and fewer people, the last being a patrol of horse police going their usual suburban round. At last we reached the churchyard, climbed the high wall with some difficulty, and found the Westenra tomb.

Van Helsing unlocked and opened the creaking bronze door. We entered the grim interior. Van Helsing took a lamp from his bag, lighting it to show the coffins with their tarnished brass fittings, the dying flowers, the dis-

coloured stone walls. We read the coffin plates and found
the bright new one that was Lucy's.

Using a turnscrew, Van Helsing opened the lid to re-
veal the lead casing beneath. Striking the turnscrew
down through the soft sheeting he made a hole large
enough to admit the point of a saw, cutting across the top
and about two feet along the sides. Taking the edge of the
loose flange, he bent it back towards the foot of the coffin,
and holding the candle over the aperture, motioned me to
look.

The coffin was empty.

My breath stuck in my throat, the shock was like a
physical blow. Van Helsing seemed unmoved, folding the
lead sheet back into place and replacing the lid. He gathered up his tools and we went outside, locking the door
behind us.

'We must now wait,' said Van Helsing. 'You must take
one side of the churchyard. I will watch the other. She
must return before daybreak. We must have patience.'

He went off and I stationed myself behind a yew tree. It was a lonely vigil. Midnight came and went, and in time, the small hours, struck off by a distant clock. It was bitterly cold and I was numb by the approach of dawn.

There was a sudden movement, a white swirl through the trees. Van Helsing had seen it too, and we moved towards it. A little way off, beyond a line of trees that marked the edge of the path that led from the church, a white, dim figure flitted in the direction of the tomb, something dark at its breast. We cut across the grass and stood side by side before the tomb.

The figure stepped from the shadow into the moonlight, saw us and stopped, hissing like a cat. It was Lucy, transformed and deadly, a small child in her arms. With a careless motion she threw the small form to the ground, her eyes bright with unholy fire. Blood ran from her mouth and dripped onto her lawn robe. She snarled and moved forward with hooked fingers as though to tear at us like an animal. Then she recoiled as Van Helsing raised his arm, holding a golden crucifix out before him.

Lucy glared for a moment, then dashed past us and threw herself at the bronze door and was gone from sight, passing through the gap between door and jamb as easily as a beam of light. The light of the dawn showed above the trees and a bird sang into the silence.

'Come, friend Jack,' ordered Van Helsing, unlocking the tomb. 'Now we can do our work.'

He threw the lid of the coffin aside and peeled back the lead sheet. The soulless face of the Thing that had been Lucy stared out at us, eyes blazing in the contorted face. Van Helsing lit candles and laid out his instruments as though preparing to save life rather than end it, methodical and careful. He handed me a sharpened wooden stake and a coal hammer.

'Place the point of the stake over the heart,' he said, 'and when I have read the prayers for the dead, you must strike with the hammer. Strike in God's name, so that the Undead will die and Lucy's soul will fly to its proper place with Him.'

Then he opened a small missal and read aloud. When he had finished I struck with all my might.

The Thing in the coffin writhed and screamed through the bloody lips, shaking and shivering in wild contortions. I struck and struck again, driving the merciful stake through the heart. The teeth ceased to champ, the face to quiver. Finally it lay still. Where a demon's mask had been were the quiet features of the Lucy we had known in life.

I sawed the top from the stake, leaving the point in the body. Van Helsing cut off the head and filled the mouth with garlic. We soldered up the lead sheet and screwed the coffin lid down. Van Helsing opened the package he had brought from the church and took out some Eucharist wafers, crumbling them and mixing the crumbs into long strips of putty, laying the strips in the crevices between the door and its setting in the tomb.

'I am closing the tomb, so that the Undead may not enter,' he explained. 'Now she is safe from the Vampire and the Devil.'

When the door was locked we tended to the child. She slept as we carried her away from there, placing her by the roadway where the next police patrol would find her. Then we went to see how our friends had fared through the night and to pursue the author of all this misery.

A shock awaited us at the Westenra house, Mina was overwrought, Lord Godalming and Quincy shaken. Jonathan had left the house soon after Van Helsing and I. He had left a note that read:

Mina, Dear Friends, I intend to find out what I can from Mr Billington of Whitby, the solicitor who acted for the Count and took the consignment of boxes from the Demeter. I shall meet you in Purfleet. We must know where those boxes lie, for they are the means by which D can find haven anywhere in the Metropolis.

Do not fear. J.

We all looked at Van Helsing whose face was calm, his eyes soft.

'Come,' he said softly, 'do we want a brave man like Jonathan to reach Jack's asylum before us? No, we must be there to welcome him.'

CHAPTER EIGHT

Jonathan Harker's Journal

I CAUGHT the night train for Yorkshire by the skin of my teeth. It seemed to stop at every halt and hamlet on the way, taking on milk and mail. I reached Whitby in the early hours of the morning and went straight away to Mr Billington's home. He was courtesy itself and, when we had breakfasted together, we went to his office where he opened his files for me, gladly showing me the documents that related to the Count's boxes. It gave me a turn to see again that man's handwriting on his letters of instruction. Mr Billington gave me copies of his orders to Carter Paterson which I took away with me.

I caught the next train to King's Cross where I sought out the station master who confirmed that the consignment had arrived there intact. From there I went to Carter Paterson's central office where I met with the utmost civility. They looked up the transaction and gave me all the details. As luck would have it, the men who had done the teaming were waiting for work and I was able to talk to them.

They remembered the dusty nature of the job, declaring that the thirst that they had worked up still lingered. We adjourned to the nearest ale house where they both swallowed the dark beer with evident enjoyment. One of the men told me:

'That there Carfax house, guvnor. The rummiest I was ever in. Blimey! Bet it ain't been touched since these hundred years. The dust lay thick as a rich man's blanket and smelled of Old Jerusalem. The old chapel took the cake. We was hard put to get out quick enough. I wouldn't take less than a quid a moment to stay there after dark.'

I left them with enough money to lay the dust and took my leave. I was mortally tired but well pleased with my discoveries. I took the train for Purfleet and a cab to Jack's asylum where Mina and my friends were waiting. Once I had told them what I had discovered they insisted that I must eat and retire for the night. I protested but gave

way and was asleep before my head touched the pillow.

I awoke the next morning quite refreshed and ate heartily with Mina and my friends. They had met as I slept, and had resolved to make a visit to Carfax House. Van Helsing had gathered a lot of equipment together and shared it out amongst us men, since we all agreed that Mina should not accompany us.

'My friends,' said Van Helsing, 'we are going into terrible danger, and we need arms of many kinds. Our enemy is not merely spiritual. He has the strength of twenty men. We cannot hurt him as he can hurt us. We must guard ourselves from his touch. You must each wear a crucifix and a garland of garlic flowers, a portion of sacred wafer for the breast pocket. For more mundane enemies, a revolver and a knife, an electric lamp to see our way. Friend Jack has many skeleton keys and we shall use them to gain access to the house. We must go at night even though Dracula is most dangerous then, for we must not be seen.'

We should have rested through the day but were all too excited and keyed up. To fill the afternoon, Doctor Seward took us on a tour of the asylum to see the poor souls in his care. One of the patients, a man called Renfield, interested Van Helsing greatly. He seemed to hear and see things that were invisible to us, and had twice run away to Carfax House and been recaptured before he could find a way inside. He pointed an accusing finger at Doctor Seward and said:

'You have kept me from my Lord and Master. I am his willing disciple. He is mighty above all. You and your thick-headed Dutchman shall not prevail against Him. He and I have consumed life.'

'What does he mean?' asked Quincy.

'His is a strange case. He is zoophagous. He eats flies and spiders. He believes that by consuming them he gains their strength. An interesting delusion.'

'No more,' said Renfield, his tone sullen, 'I am tired of their tiny souls buzzing in my ears. The Master has shown me bigger game.'

'Guard this man well, Jack,' Van Helsing said to Doctor Seward. 'He can only mean one man. Dracula himself.'

The attendant that accompanied us took Doctor Se-

ward to one side and spoke to him confidentially. Jack turned quite pale. He ordered Renfield's door locked and led us back to his study where he carefully closed the door.

'My attendant has given me some disquieting information,' said Jack. 'Renfield escaped from his nurse whilst we were away yesterday. He was found attacking two carters outside Carfax House. One of the men had to fell him with his whip. The men were removing boxes from the old chapel. The men were given a sovereign each to stop them suing for assault. My man has their names.'

A silence fell over the room.

'The evil has begun to spread,' said Van Helsing. 'May night fall quickly.'

The moon showed through fitful clouds as we left the asylum and made our way to the path that led to the grounds of Carfax House. Mist clung to the ground and the dark lake with its ring of old willows was noisy with frogs. We reached the great door of the old house and Doctor Seward tried one or two skeleton keys, his mechanical dexterity as a surgeon standing him in good stead. Presently the bolt yielded and with a rusty clang, shot back. We pressed on the door, the rusty hinges creaked, and it slowly opened. The Professor was first to move forward, and stepped through into the darkness.

'*In manus tuas, Domine!*' he said, crossing himself as he passed over the threshold.

The light from our electric lamps picked out odd details and threw great shadows. I was reminded of my surroundings in Transylvania, all of us looked over our shoulders at every sound and every new shadow. The whole place was thick with dust. In the corners were masses of spiders' webs, hanging like tattered rags. A bunch of labelled keys lay on the hall table. Van Helsing took them up and turned to me.

'You know this place, Jonathan. You have copied maps of it. Which is the way to the chapel?'

I led the way, and after a few wrong turnings found myself opposite a low, arched oaken door, ribbed with iron bands. With a little trouble we found the right key and opened the door. None of us expected the foul odour we encountered. The place was small and close and the long

disuse made the air stagnant, heavy with corruption, acrid with the smell of blood. Every breath exhaled by that monster seemed to have clung to the place and intensified its loathsomeness. Only our high and terrible purpose gave us the strength to face the appalling stench.

The black boxes lay in silent rows. There were only twenty-nine left out of the fifty! Lord Godalming turned suddenly to stare out of the vaulted door into the dark passage beyond. I seemed to see the Count's evil face, the ridged nose, the red eyes set in the awful pallor, but it was only the shadows. Fear had helped our imagination for there was no hiding place, even for him.

Quincy stepped away from the corner he was examining and we all instinctively drew back. Phosphorescence twinkled like stars. The whole place was becoming alive with rats. For a moment we stood appalled, all save Lord Godalming, who rushed to the door and blew a whistle, a low, shrill call. It was answered from behind Doctor Seward's house by the yelping of dogs. The rats swarmed everywhere, their eyes glittering in the lamplight. The dogs, three terriers, dashed up to the door and stopped dead, lifting their muzzles and howling dismally.

Lord Godalming lifted one of the dogs and set him inside. The instant his feet touched the floor he recovered his courage and rushed at his natural enemies. Lord Godalming lifted the other terriers in and they joined in the massacre. The rats melted away as if they had never been. The terriers romped and frisked, tossing the dead rats into the air. The shadow of dread lifted from us as we watched the dogs sporting merrily. We set to with hammers and smashed each one of the boxes, spilling the mould out and trampling it underfoot. Dracula could never again take refuge in this district.

We went out into the fresh air of the quickening dawn. Our work had taken longer than I imagined. Van Helsing was thoughtful as we returned to the asylum. He stopped suddenly as we walked up the front steps, looking at me hard.

'We have seen our enemy's power over the beasts. He had set those rats to guard his domain. He would have faced us himself if he had not been elsewhere. Look to your wife, Jonathan.'

I raced into the house and up the stairs to our bedroom, Lord Godalming and Quincy close behind me. I threw open the door. The room seemed to be filled with fog, darker near the bed. A dark form leaned over Mina. I leapt forward, holding my crucifix out ahead of me. The face of Dracula stared at me out of the swirl, his mouth snarling. The fog around him writhed away from the cross. Then he was gone through the open window. I looked down at Mina's sleeping form. Two small holes showed on her white neck. I sank down on the bed staring helplessly as Van Helsing tended to her.

'We were in time, Jonathan my friend. He has not harmed her too much. But we must see that he cannot approach her again,' he said.

'Can we destroy this foul thing?' I asked. 'Are we strong enough?'

'God pray that we are,' said Arthur.

'We must follow hard on his heels,' said Quincy. 'He must be allowed no rest, no respite from our pursuit.'

'Amen to that,' said Jack Seward. 'I will get the names of those carters from my attendant. Then off to London.'

From the far end of the building, a voice I recognised as

belonging to Renfield started to rail.

'Your foul work has angered the Master. You have sealed your doom. He will return and take his revenge!'

CHAPTER NINE

Jonathan Harker's Journal

I FOUND one of the carters in Bethnal Green where he had just returned from a night of heavy drinking and he could not answer my questions. His poor wife gave me the address of the driver he worked for, her drunken husband being only his assistant. I drove to Walworth where I found Joseph Smollet at home in his shirt-sleeves, taking tea from a saucer. This reliable man remembered the job and consulted his notebook. He had taken six boxes from Carfax to 197 Chicksand Street, Mile End, and another six boxes to Jamaica Lane, Bermondsey.

I asked him if he knew of another carter who had taken such a load from Carfax, giving him half a guinea to refresh his memory.

'Well, guv'nor,' he said, 'I heard a man by the name of Bloxham say how he'd had a rare dusty old job in Purfleet. There ain't so many jobs of the like that you'd waste your time talking to Sam Bloxham.'

I thanked him and asked where Bloxham could be found.

'Sam's a rare man for the drink,' said Smollet. 'He's known to sup at the Hare and Hounds in Pincher's Alley. But he's off early of a morning, drink or no drink. If you was to leave me your address I could search him out and get you word.'

I gave him another half-guinea and he promised to start his search straight away. His letter arrived at Purfleet by the morning post, written with a carpenter's scrawling hand:

Sam Bloxham, 4 Potters Court, Walworth.

After telling my friends where I was going, I went there and found it to be a lodging house, the door being answered by a surly fellow who told me that Bloxham had left for work at five in the morning. He could not tell me more than that his place of work was a 'new-fangled warehouse' in Poplar. It was noon before I found some workmen in a coffee house who gave me a clue to what I was looking for. One of them suggested that the new cold-store in Cross Angel Street might be the place I sought.

A half-crown in the palm of the gatekeeper and another in the hand of the foreman gained me an interview with Bloxham. We settled on a guinea for the information I wanted. He had made two journeys between Carfax and a house in Piccadilly, carrying nine boxes with a horse and cart that he had hired for that purpose. He couldn't remember the number of the house. He said:

'It was only a few doors along from a big white church not long built. A dusty old house too, but not so dusty as Carfax.'

'How did you get into the house if they were both empty?'

'The old party what hired me was a-waiting in the house at Purfleet. He gave me a lift with the boxes. Curse me, if he wasn't the strongest chap I ever struck. He took his end of them boxes as if they was pounds of tea, and me puffing and blowing before I got mine shifted an inch. And I ain't no chicken neither.'

'How did you get into the Piccadilly house?' I asked.

'He was there too. He must have started off and got there afore me, for when I rung the bell there he was.'

'And you can't remember the number of the house?'

'No, sir. But you can't miss it. It's a high one with a stone front with a bow to it. And high steps up to the front door.'

I thanked him and took my cab on to Piccadilly where I discharged it. Walking westward, I came across the house. It looked untenanted, the windows encrusted with dirt, the paint flaking from the railings. I walked around to the mews at the rear and asked the grooms and helpers what they knew of the empty house. None of them knew who had purchased the property, but one remembered that the agents were Mitchell, Sons & Candy of Sackville Street.

I was soon in their offices where I saw a very haughty gentleman who had no intention of telling me who had bought the house. I gave him my card and told him that

I acted for Lord Godalming. His change of manner was nothing short of miraculous.

'I should like to oblige his lordship. If you will tell me where I can write to him I will communicate the information gladly.'

I thanked him and gave Doctor Seward's address. It was now dark, and I was tired and hungry. I got a cup of tea at the Aerated Bread Company and took the next train to Purfleet.

I found all the others at home. Mina had stayed upstairs, complaining of feeling unwell. My three friends had been back to Carfax and sprinkled the chapel with holy water, sterilising the mould. I told them what I had discovered in London, and asked Lord Godalming to forgive me for using his title at the estate agents. He congratulated me on my presence of mind.

'That information is vital to us, Jonathan,' he said, 'for it will pinpoint the final lair of Dracula.'

'We shall destroy the boxes in the houses in Mile End and Bermondsey when we are sure that the Piccadilly house is where the last of the boxes lie. Then, Dracula will have to return there at dawn. And we, my friends, will be waiting for him,' said Van Helsing. He laid a hand on my arm and gently added: 'You have done glorious work this day. But you must rest my young friend.'

I bid my friends goodnight and went up to the bedroom. Mina was asleep. She did not wake as I checked the garlic around the locked window and prepared myself for sleep.

CHAPTER TEN

Doctor Jack Seward's Journal

JONATHAN's detective work in London had brightened us, and we sat smoking cigars over good brandy before retiring. Van Helsing smiled for the first time in days as Quincy entertained us with stories of his travels in South America. Then the door burst open and one of my attendants entered to tell me that there had been an accident in the patient's wing. Renfield was badly injured. We all went to his room where

he lay on his side in a spreading pool of blood. His face was horribly bruised as though it had been beaten against the floor.

'I think, sir, that his back is broken,' said the attendant. 'His whole right side is paralysed. How this has happened is a mystery.'

Van Helsing and I exchanged glances full of meaning, for this could have been no accident. I sent the attendant away so that we could speak more freely. Renfield's facial cuts were superficial; the real injury was a depressed fracture of the skull. It was clear that we must fix the best spot for trephining to remove the blood clot, for the haemorrhage was increasing. Van Helsing's face was sternly set as he said:

'There is no time to lose. His words may save many lives. There may be a soul at stake. We shall operate just above the ear.'

Without another word he made the operation. For a few moments there was no change in Renfield's harsh breathing, then his eyes opened, fixed in a wild, helpless stare.

'What happened, Renfield?' I asked, giving him a little brandy.

'It was no nightmare, no dream,' he said painfully. 'My mind is clear. I know that I am dying at His hand. The Master came to the window last night, wrapped in mist. I knew that He could not enter until I invited Him. He promised me such wondrous things.'

'What did he promise you, Renfield?' asked Van Helsing.

'Lives, millions of lives. He called me to the window, and as I looked out, He raised his hands, calling without words. A dark mass spread out over the grass, thousands of rats with their eyes blazing red. Like His, only smaller. He held up his hand and they stopped. He seemed to be saying: "All these lives will I give you through the countless ages if you will worship me." I said: "Come in, Master," and He came in like mist. Then Mrs Harker was in the room with us and I slept.'

Renfield coughed and licked his dry lips. I dipped a handkerchief in brandy and wiped his lips with it. He could not last much longer.

'So that is how he got into the house despite our defences,' said Van Helsing. 'That is hard news indeed.'

'He came again tonight,' said Renfield. 'I asked Him for my rats. He would not give them to me. He wanted only to drink the life from Mrs. Harker. He was turning again to mist. I grasped him and held him. I had to stop Him from taking more of her life, for he would not give me my lives. Then His eyes burned at me and my strength turned to water. He raised me up and flung me down. There was a red cloud and thunder and the mist stole away under the door.'

'My God,' said Quincy. 'He is in the house!'

'Mina,' said Lord Godalming.

We rushed down the passage and along to the main building and threw ourselves against the bedroom door, smashing it open and sprawling inside. What I saw appalled me. The hair on the back of my neck stood on end.

In the bright yellow moonlight the room was as bright as day. Jonathan lay on the floor. Dracula stood next to Mina, holding her mouth onto her husband's neck. Dracula's eyes flamed red, his nostrils quivering. He

threw Mina from him and leapt at us. Van Helsing held
out his crucifix and the sacred wafer. The Count reared
away as though burned, cowering. We all lifted our
crucifixes and advanced. There was a sudden fog in the
room that writhed out through the open door and
Dracula was gone.

Mina threw back her head and screamed, her eyes mad
with terror. Lord Godalming and Quincy whirled around
and pounded off down the passage in pursuit as Van Helsing and I did what we could to calm Mina and revive
Jonathan.

Mina fell into the Professor's arms and wept bitterly as
he spoke gently, smoothing her tumbled hair.

'Have courage,' he said, 'do not despair.'

'I have no will to live,' mourned Mina. 'I have tainted my husband with my foul lips. I must die!'

'Put that thought from you,' ordered Van Helsing. 'If you die you would be one of his Undead. Believe in the true faith and live to see the fiend perish.'

'He made me go to him,' sobbed Mina. 'He said mockingly: "You, their beloved one, now belong to me. You are flesh of my flesh and blood of my blood. You shall come to my call, cross land and sea to do my bidding." 'God pity me, I know his very thoughts.'

'That may help us, Madame Mina,' said Van Helsing. 'If you know his thoughts I can mesmerise you and hear what he is doing from your lips. See, your husband is revived and knows you.'

Mina clung to Jonathan who had no memory of what had gone before. He was angry when he was told. Quincy and Lord Godalming came back and told us that Dracula had left the way that he had come and that Renfield was dead. They had used their garlands of garlic to shield the window.

'We have to leave now,' said Jonathan. 'Smash the boxes in the East End and then lie in wait at Piccadilly.'

'No, my young friend,' said Van Helsing. 'Dracula has fed well this night and will go to rest. We have time to rest ourselves, for he will not travel until nightfall tomorrow. Mina must be protected. See, I place this sacred wafer on her wounded neck.'

As the wafer touched Mina's neck she stiffened, groaned deeply and fainted dead away. The flesh where the wafer had touched it was scalded a bright crimson.

'I care for nothing now,' said Jonathan, 'except to wipe this brute from the face of creation. I would sell my soul to do it.'

'Hush, my young friend,' said Van Helsing. 'God does not buy souls in this way; and the Devil, though he may purchase, does not keep faith. We shall wait for the morning, then we shall split into two groups. Lord Arthur, Jack and Quincy will go to the East End, you, Mina and I will go to Piccadilly. Madame Mina may tell us where Dracula is if we can use her new power properly.'

CHAPTER ELEVEN

Jonathan Harker's Journal

THE letter from the estate agent arrived and Lord Arthur read it to us before we took the train to London. It read as follows:

My Lord, With regard to the desire of your Lordship, expressed by Mr Harker on your behalf, to supply the following information concerning the sale and purchase of No. 347 Piccadilly. The vendor was Mr Archibald Winter-Suffield. The purchaser is a foreign nobleman, Count de Ville, who made the purchase in cash. Beyond this we know nothing of him.

Yr. Lordship's humble servants,
MITCHELL, SONS & CANDY.

Quincy laughed aloud, slapping his thigh. 'That is the man or I'm mistaken,' he said. 'By the powers, Lord Arthur, Jack and I will be quick in our work and join you in Piccadilly soon after noon.'

'I think that we will all go to Piccadilly, Quincy,' said Lord Arthur. 'The use of my title will enable us to get a locksmith easily. When we have opened the house and seen that it is safe, we will leave Professor Van Helsing, Jonathan and Mina there. They should be safe until we return.'

We all agreed to this and set off.

When we arrived at Fenchurch Street we took two cabs to Piccadilly where our party set down by Green Park, Lord Arthur and Quincy driving on to find a locksmith. The minutes seemed to pass with leaden feet as we waited for their return.

When their cab returned, Lord Arthur and Quincy got out in a leisurely fashion, a workman climbing down from the box. Quincy paid off the cab and the three of them mounted the steps of the house where the workman set to work after hanging his coat on the railings. A passing policeman stopped to talk, then touching a finger to his helmet, moved away. The door was opened in moments

and when Lord Godalming had paid the workman, he and Quincy entered the building as if they owned it.

When the workman was safely out of sight we four crossed the road and knocked at the door. It was immediately opened by Quincy Morris, beside whom stood Lord Godalming lighting a cigar. He said coolly, 'The place smells vile. It is plain that the Count has used it freely.'

We moved through the house cautiously, keeping together in case of attack, for we had no way of knowing whether the Count was in the house or not. In the dining room we found the nine great boxes. We opened the shutters and looked out on a flagged yard that backed onto the blind wall of a stable. None of the other rooms, from

cellar to attic, had been used. All the Count's effects were in one room, heaped carelessly on the dining room table. The deeds for this house and the two in the East End, notepaper, ink and pens, many gold coins, a toilet set, and a jug and basin, the latter containing dirty water reddened with blood. Last of all was a small heap of keys, carefully labelled.

Then we set to work destroying all the boxes save one that stood at the centre of the room. Quincy and Lord Arthur selected the keys that opened the houses in the East End, gathered up the tools that they would need to destroy any boxes they found, and left us. Then we waited, the hardest hours of my life.

Mina sat between us men, a thin bowed figure who seemed not to be aware of our presence, as though listening to something far off. I stayed close to her and my two medical friends watched her closely. We started a fire in the grate and burned all the Count's papers, without which he would have no title to his properties. Just before sundown, Mina cocked her head on one side and spoke in a sighing voice.

'He feels the destruction,' she said. 'He knows that he must . . . come here.'

'What is this?' I asked.

'She has contact with the Count's mind,' explained Van Helsing. 'She knows his thoughts. It seems our friends have been successful. The Count will be afoot like mortal men. His power will be diminished as each of his graves is sterilised. He must come against us before sundown, not as a wolf or bat, but in his human form. He must reach this last resting place to renew his strength before he can transform himself to any beastly form. Pray that our friends reach us first.'

A quiet knock at the front door had me on my feet, my pistol in one hand, my crucifix in the other. Van Helsing went along the passage and opened the door. Lord Arthur and Quincy came in quickly, their faces triumphant.

'It is all right,' said Quincy. 'We found both places; six boxes in each, and we destroyed them all.'

'There were no other effects in either house,' said Lord Arthur.

'Then this must be his chief location,' said Jack Seward, his eyes bright. 'We must be ready for him.'

'Water,' whispered Mina, 'the tide is slack. He has passed over. There is foul anger in him. And darkness.'

'That means you must have been at Bermondsey only a short time before him. That he is not already here shows that he went to Mile End next,' said Van Helsing. 'Be ready, for he cannot be long.'

Quincy took charge and placed us in strategic positions around the room, setting Mina well out of the way behind the upturned table. He held up a warning hand, and we all heard a key softly inserted in the front door lock.

We waited in suspense that made the seconds pass with nightmare slowness. The slow, careful steps came along

the hall, cautious and catlike. With a single bound the familiar black figure was in the room, winning a way past us before we could raise a hand to stop him. He turned in a slow half-circle as he glared at us each in turn. His face was drawn into a snarl, the scar I had given him a livid stripe on his white forehead. His eyes shone as though lit from behind, his eyeteeth as long and as sharp as tusks.

I leapt to the door of the room, slamming it shut. The Count slashed out at me with his long nails and I countered by firing my pistol at his chest. His waxen face took on a greenish cast in contrast to his burning eyes as blood showed against the rusty black of his waistcoat. He knocked the gun from my hand, sending me spinning with a blow from his forearm. I crashed against the far wall and dropped to the ground totally winded.

Quincy leapt in, slashing with his bowie knife, raking the Count's coat. Paper money and coins spilled from the slashed pocket, the gold chiming as it struck the marble floor. Dracula took Quincy by the lapels and hurled him away across the smashed boxes. Then the slender figure of Van Helsing was between them, a bottle in his hand. He brought it down on the Count's shoulder, shattering it into a thousand pieces, the liquid inside dousing Dracula's arms and torso. It was the remains of the Holy Water.

The Count screamed like a great beast as his clothes
began to smoke, the flesh beneath to bubble. He made a
great leap across the Professor, up onto the black box,
crouching at bay, howling. The air around him was filled
with a strange whirling light.

The Count held out his hand to Mina, drawing her from
her place of hiding with sheer willpower. She stumbled
forward, her face blank. I could not reach her.

Jack Seward jumped from behind Dracula and threw
himself across Mina, bearing her to the floor, holding his
crucifix above them both. The Count recoiled, taking a

step backwards. Quincy stepped up to him and drove his knife into Dracula's heart. The Count fell to his knees and seemed to be crumbling to dust, his body falling in on itself, just the flaming eyes staring out of his skull. Then they flared and were gone as if they had never been.

I went across to Mina just as Jack was helping her to her feet.

The setting sun glowed through the window, illuminating her. Her eyes were soft and loving as she smiled at me, the awful stigmata on her neck completely gone.

We had triumphed after all.